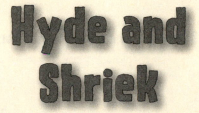

Hyde and Shriek

Hyde and Shriek

A MONSTERRIFIC TALE

DAVID LUBAR

A Tom Doherty Associates Book
New York

HYDE AND SHRIEK

Copyright © 2012 by David Lubar

The Vanishing Vampire excerpt copyright © 1997 by David Lubar

Illustrations by Marcos Calo

A Starscape Book
Published by Tom Doherty Associates, LLC
175 Fifth Avenue
New York, NY 10010

www.tor-forge.com

Library of Congress Cataloging-in-Publication Data

Lubar, David.
    Hyde and shriek / David Lubar. — 1st ed.
        p. cm.
    "A Tom Doherty Associates Book."
    ISBN 978-0-7653-3081-9 (hardcover)
    ISBN 978-1-4299-9312-8 (e-book)
    1. Teachers—Fiction.   2. Schools—Fiction.
3. Shapeshifting—Fiction.   4. Science fiction.   I. Stevenson,
Robert Louis, 1850–1894. Strange case of Dr. Jekyll &
Mr. Hyde.   II. Title.
    PZ7.L96775Hyd 2013
    [Fic]—dc23
                                                      2012024889

First Edition: January 2013

0 9 8 7 6 5 4 3 2 1

For Stoker, Stevenson,
Shelley, and all the others
who laid the trail

Contents

Author's Note

I've always been a fan of monsters. As a kid, I watched monster movies, read monster magazines, built monster models, and even tried my hand at monster makeup for Halloween. Basically, I was a creepy little kid. It's no surprise that, when I grew up and became a writer, I would tell monster stories. I've written a lot of them over the years. My short-story collections, such as *Attack of the Vampire Weenies and Other Warped and Creepy Tales*, are full of vampires, werewolves, ghosts, witches, giant insects, and other classic creatures. The book you hold in your hands is also about a monster. But it is different from my short stories in a wonderful way. Let me explain.

Years ago, I decided I wanted to tell a tale through the eyes of a monster. That idea excited me, but it didn't feel special enough by itself. Then, I had a second idea that went perfectly with the first one. What if a kid became a monster? Even better—what if the kid had to decide whether to remain a monster, or to become human again? The result of these ideas was not one book, but six. It seems the town of Lewington attracts a monsteriffic amount of trouble. To find out more, read on.

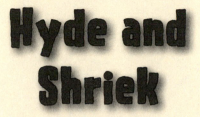

Hyde and Shriek

One

AN IMPORTANT MEAL

I love kids. They make great hood ornaments. No. Stop that. Be good. Be nice. Okay. I'm back in control. That was a terrible thing to say. It was mean and sick and nasty. Not like me at all. I don't know where it came from.

Yes, I do.

But it won't happen again. I'm a teacher. And a scientist. I can control myself. I'm a trained, professional teacher. Miss Clevis. That's what the students call me. That's what it says on the door to my room. My whole name is Jackie Jean Clevis. I teach science at Washington Irving Elementary School in Lewington.

But something funny happened to me this morning.

I was making breakfast. And I was getting a batch of chemicals ready to take to class for an experiment. *Be very careful with chemicals.* That's the first thing I tell the students. I was also listening to the news on the radio, and I was thinking about the science fair, and I was looking out the window at some lovely nimbus clouds. The science fair is scheduled for next weekend, and I'm in charge. Which makes sense, since I'm the science teacher. It's a lot of work, and it's very important.

So, between breakfast and the experiment, and the radio and the science fair and the clouds, it wouldn't have been impossible for me to accidentally put the wrong ingredients in the blender when I made my banana-honey-yogurt morning breakfast drink.

I'm pretty sure that's what happened. I don't usually pass out right after breakfast. I don't usually pass out at all. But one moment I was drinking my drink and tuning the station on the radio, and staring out the window. The next thing I knew, I was on the floor, surrounded by broken pieces of my drinking glass. I didn't even remember hitting the floor.

I sat on the floor for a minute, trying to see whether I'd bruised or broken anything besides the glass. But everything seemed fine. Then I noticed the clock. Oh, dear. I was late for school. I'd been lying there for at least ten minutes. I grabbed the chemicals, put them in a box, got my briefcase, and rushed out the door.

As I tossed everything in my car, I thought about

what had just happened. There were so many possible explanations, it was pointless to try to guess the right one. As long as it didn't happen again, I wasn't going to worry. I had other things on my mind. I felt fine now. Otherwise, I wouldn't have gotten behind the wheel of my car. Safety first, I always say. In the lab or on the road, safety has to come first.

At the corner by the stop sign at Maynard and Brockton, I got stuck behind someone who took a long time making a left turn. I didn't mind waiting. But some idiot started honking his horn. I looked behind me. There was nobody there. Who was honking? The sound was getting very annoying. I looked down at my right hand. Oh my goodness. It was me who was banging on the horn. I hadn't even realized I was doing anything.

I pulled my hand back. This wasn't like me. I never use my horn. I'm very patient. You have to be patient to teach. Patient and caring and kind. I gripped the wheel very hard for the rest of the trip, just to make sure I didn't use the horn again.

I got to school and parked in the teachers' lot, then went up to my classroom on the second floor. "Hi, Jackie," Mr. Rubinitski said as I walked down the hall. He teaches sixth grade. There are three sixth-grade teachers. They handle math and English and social studies. The kids switch around for the different subjects. But I do all the science classes.

"Good morning, Chester." I smiled at him. We had

16

a great staff at Why. That's what we called it. We abbreviate Washington Irving Elementary to WIE, but we pronounce it *Why*. It's sort of our own little private joke.

Where do you teach?

Why.

No, I asked where you teach.

I told you: Why.

We sort of stole the idea from an old comedy routine. We use it each year in a skit when we have our teachers' lunch. And they say teachers don't have a sense of humor.

I went into my room and put down the box of chemicals.

Thwump! Thawump!

A sharp, slapping sound caused me to look across the room. There, hovering in a cloud, was a figure with a face as white as death. He let out an awful, gasping wheeze.

Two

BITE THE DUST

"Norman," I asked, "what are you doing here?"

Thawump!

"I wanted to come in early and clean the chalk erasers for you," he said. Then he coughed and wheezed some more. He was covered with chalk dust.

"I appreciate that," I told him. "But maybe you should go out and get some fresh air."

He nodded, wheezed again, then walked toward the door. At the edge, he stopped and said, "Miss Clevis, I was wondering about the science fair. You know how you said I couldn't do any more projects that might explode? Well, could you make a tiny little exception this time? I'm really fascinated by nuclear energy. So I started working on this project. And I know I should have asked permission sooner, but I sort of got wrapped up in it."

I glanced across the classroom to the part of the wall that had to be rebuilt after Norman's internal combustion engine had overheated last year. Then I looked up at the ceiling at the spot he'd melted the year before last with his homemade laser. Then I glanced down at the floor. He'd blasted a chunk out of it in third grade when his radio-controlled jackhammer went out of radio control. I couldn't remember what he'd destroyed in second grade, but I was sure it had been some part of the room.

"Well, can I bring a nuclear reactor to the science fair?" he asked.

I opened my mouth to say *absolutely not,* but what came out was, "Why sure, Norman. Radioactive devices would be fine. The more, the better."

"Thanks!" He was out the door before I could catch him.

I couldn't believe I'd just given him permission for that. But there was nothing to be done about it at the moment. I stopped worrying about Norman and started getting ready for my first class. I had one of the kindergarten classes this morning. It's never too early to teach science. We didn't do much, but we had fun. This is a very progressive school.

I was excited about the class because I'd planned a

special treat for them. It was an old science teachers' trick. I had a simple chemical that created a wonderful imitation of a volcano. It threw up a shower of sparks and produced a green ash that looked like flowing lava. I knew the kids would love it.

The bell for first period rang. After a few minutes, Mrs. Rubric came in with her class. The kids looked so cute as they found seats.

"Is everyone ready for something special?" I asked the class.

"Yes, Miss Clevis," they called out.

"Well, good." I clapped my hands together, then held up the jar filled with orange crystals. "We're going to use this special chemical to make—" I paused and looked around at them, then said the magic words. "—a volcano."

This produced a lot of *Ooooooohhhh*s and *Yaaaayy*s. I had a small clay volcano on the table. I put a piece of paper in the opening at the top of the volcano, then poured out the chemical until it covered everything but the tip of the paper. After I closed up the jar, I walked across the room to turn off the room lights. Then I pulled the shades. It was nice and dark—perfect for a volcano.

All the students got very quiet when I lit the match. They hunched forward, their little faces filled with anticipation. "Watch this," I said, feeling as much like a magician as I did a scientist.

I lit the paper fuse. The flame crept toward the orange crystals. In a moment, the fire ignited the chemical and the show began. Bright yellow sparks flew up in a shower and green ashes overflowed the crater at the top of the volcano, running down the sides like streams of lava.

I smiled and leaned over the volcano, being careful not to get too close to the sparks. Then I glanced toward the children, eager to see the look of awe and excitement in their bright, happy faces.

There's nothing so wonderful as a simple science experiment. And this one always pleased the kids.

When I looked out at them, they started to scream. First one, then two, then almost all of them screamed, their little voices filling the air with a sound like a thousand whistling teakettles. As I stood there, frozen, most of the children leaped from their seats and rushed down the hall, still screaming.

Three

SOMETHING ISN'T RIGHT

I stood there, not knowing what to do. The kids were supposed to go *Oooooohhhh* or *Cool* or *Wow*. They weren't supposed to run screaming in terror. Across the room, Mrs. Rubric flipped on the lights. I looked at her.

"What's going on?" I asked.

She shrugged and smiled nervously. "I'd better go round them up," she said. She dashed off. In my mind, I could almost see her riding a horse and whirling a lasso over her head as she herded the kindergartners back to the corral. *Round them up*. What a phrase.

The few kids who were still in their seats stared at me with fear-filled eyes. As I took a step toward them, a girl leaped up and screamed, "Wait for me!" She went tearing down the hall after her teacher.

One boy looked calmer than the rest. He also looked familiar. "You're Sebastian's brother, aren't you?" I asked.

He nodded.

Sebastian was in my sixth-grade class. He was a bit of a clown and a show-off, but he had a good heart. "What's your name?" I asked him.

"Rory," he said.

"Well, Rory, do you have any idea why all those boys and girls left the room?"

He nodded.

"That's great. Do you think you could tell me?"

He nodded again.

"Do you think you could tell me now?"

Another nod. "Promise not to get mad?" he asked.

"I promise."

He looked around the room. I waited as patiently as I could, wondering if he was going to run off, too. Finally, he spoke. "You looked real scary."

"What?"

"Leaning over the volcano. Dad does that on Halloween. He puts a flashlight under his chin. The light makes him look spooky. I don't get too scared, since I know it's Dad. But I get a little bit scared."

I realized that, with the orange glow of the volcano

shining up at my face in the dark room, I might have looked the same way. "So I was spooky, Rory? Is that it?"

"Sorta . . . ," he said. "But . . . don't get mad . . . okay? You looked bad spooky. Not fun spooky." He paused and stared up at me, then asked, "You mad?"

I shook my head and smiled. Young children have such a wonderful way with words. *Bad spooky.* My smile grew wider. Then I laughed. Rory closed his eyes when I did that. In my ears, I heard the echo of my laugh. It wasn't a chuckle or a giggle. It was a spooky laugh. *Bad spooky.*

"Maybe you'd better go join your class," I said.

Rory nodded and got up. The other kids who were still in the room dashed off after him.

This was terrible. How could I teach children if I scared them? Teaching was my life. But it was ridiculous to worry about something that had never happened before and would probably never happen again. I was sure it was just an odd accident of the lighting in the room. At worst, I'd have to make sure I didn't stand over the volcano the next time. I certainly didn't want to scare more children. But when I thought about them running and screaming in fear, something made me grin.

I put those thoughts aside, realizing that I was still a little dizzy from my breakfast drink. It would pass.

The rest of the morning went normally. I didn't

terrify anyone else. Of course, I had mostly sixth-graders, and just about nothing terrifies them.

Then, right before lunch, my normal world was torn apart. And so was I.

Four

JACKIE

As I was getting ready for lunch, Mr. Rubinitski stuck his head in my room and said, "Hi. Got a second?"

"Sure," I said, waving him in.

He came over to my desk and put something down. "I was out of town this weekend, and I saw this in a museum shop. I figured you'd like it."

"Thanks. I love fossils." I picked it up and examined it. "You shouldn't have."

"My pleasure," he said. "Well, I'd better get going." He smiled and walked off.

I held the fossil for a moment, then put it down and dropped back into my chair as another wave of dizziness washed over me. It was much worse than before. But then, just as suddenly, I felt fine.

Goodness.

"It's gone," I said to myself. The dizziness was completely gone. I stood up cautiously, but everything was fine. Better than fine. I felt great—just in time for lunch. As I walked through the empty classroom, I noticed something else. The room was different. It had grown bigger. No, not bigger. Taller. Everything was taller. Not by much. But enough for me to notice.

Something weird was going on.

But I didn't care. I felt fabulous. I walked out to the hall. Wait. I wasn't walking. Goodness. I was skipping. I hadn't done that in years. When I realized what I was doing, I giggled. My word—I couldn't remember the last time I'd giggled, either. What next? I wondered.

"Hi."

I turned toward the voice. It was Dawn, a sixth-grader. One of my favorite students. She was always so nice and cheerful. What a lovely girl.

"Hi," I said back. I was about to ask her if she was ready for the science fair when she spoke again.

"You must be new," she said, staring at me. "My name's Dawn."

I didn't answer. It wasn't just her words that froze me. It was her eyes. They were level with mine. I glanced down at my feet. I still had my shoes, though they looked a bit large. I checked Dawn's feet. Sneak-

28

ers. Dawn was tall for a sixth-grader, but I'd always been taller. Until now. Somehow, I'd lost two or three inches. I checked the hem of my skirt. It was definitely lower than before. Goodness gracious.

"What's your name?" Dawn asked.

"Jackie," I said.

"You look familiar," Dawn told me. "Come on—I'll show you where the cafeteria is."

"Thanks." I followed Dawn downstairs. We went to the end of the hall and around the corner. As we walked past the auditorium, I caught sight of my reflection in the glass front of a display case. Oh my goodness. I couldn't help gasping. This was wonderful. I looked like I was eleven again. I felt great, too.

"Come on," Dawn urged. "It's burger day. If we're late, we'll get the burgers from the bottom of the pan. You know—the ones that have meat goo around the edges."

"Can't risk meat goo," I said, hurrying after Dawn. Sure, I had things to figure out, like why I'd turned into a kid. But right now, I just wanted to enjoy lunch. People spent too much time worrying. And too little time enjoying the pleasures of life. Too much meat goo, not enough meat.

"Where are you from?" Dawn asked as we got into the lunch line.

"I grew up in Denver," I said. That was certainly true. I'd grown up there, and now I'd grown down.

"I've never been to Denver," Dawn said. "I'd like to go someday. There are lots of places I'd like to see."

I got my burger—no goo—and paid with the money I had in my skirt pocket. Then I followed Dawn to a table where we joined four other girls.

"This is Jackie," Dawn said. "From Denver." She pointed around the table and named her friends, "Kim, Nicole, Rose, and Brittany."

We all said hi to one another. I waited for one of the girls to recognize me.

"You look familiar," Kim said.

"A lot of people say that to me," I told her. And that was as far as it went. At the next table, I noticed Norman and Sebastian. Norman was reading a chemistry book and writing notes on a piece of paper. Sebastian was sticking straws in his nose and humming.

"Ignore him," Dawn said. "He's trying to impress us. If you pay any attention, he'll start getting real silly."

I looked away from Sebastian, though I was tempted to find out how silly he could become.

Maybe I should have been worried about the change that had just happened to me, but that didn't seem important right now. I figured I'd change back eventually. For the moment, I wasn't concerned. It didn't do any good to worry.

Besides—lunch was fascinating. It turned out that one of the students' favorite subject was teachers. At first, they talked about the ones they liked. It was wonderful to hear them say nice things about my fellow teachers. I tried not to listen when they said nice things about Miss Clevis—I mean, about me. It felt too much like I was spying. Still, it was good to hear that they liked science. But then, things turned nasty.

"I hate Mr. Brickner," Nicole said.

"Yeah." Rose nodded. "He's so mean."

That shocked me. How could they think sweet old Mr. Brickner, who was ancient enough to remember most of the history he was teaching, could be mean? He always looked so gentle, walking down the hall in his faded tan suit and brown tie, clutching the handle of the battered old cane he carried everywhere. I thought he was very charming. Instead of joining the conversation, I took a bite of my burger and chewed it slowly.

Goodness. The meat tasted wonderful. I took a gulp of cold milk. That tasted great, too. Kim passed me one of the cookies her mother had baked. What a perfect way to end my meal.

A bell rang. Around me, everyone stood up and started to leave the cafeteria.

"Do you know where you're going?" Dawn asked. "I can help you find your next class."

"I'm fine," I said. "Thanks for being so nice."

She smiled. "Okay, see you later."

I felt too good to move just yet. Lunch had really been just about perfect. The taste of the cookie lingered

31

in my mouth. I sighed, closed my eyes, and sat back in my seat.

Whack!

I jumped.

"Get moving!"

I turned toward the shout.

Whack!

Mr. Brickner's cane rose and fell as he smacked the table after each sentence. "Don't dillydally, young lady. This is not a resort hotel. This is a school. *S-c-h-o-o-l*. Get moving. Now."

"Yes, sir," I said, scrambling away from the table and hurrying into the hall.

Where all my goodness left me.

Five

MS. HYDE

Curses!

The stupid dizziness made me stumble, but just for a step or two. Then my head cleared. Where was I? I looked around. The hall was lined with pictures drawn by children. Crayon pictures of animals. How disgusting. Didn't children have anything better to do than draw? What a waste of time.

"Can I help you?"

I spun toward the voice. It was Mr. Rubinitski. How nice. He wanted to help me. Well, I didn't need anybody's help. I didn't want anybody's help. But if I didn't explain who I was, I knew there could be trouble. And

I didn't want trouble, unless I was the one who made it. Obviously, he didn't recognize me. I'd changed, somehow. It didn't matter how or why I'd changed. I could tell from the way I felt that I'd changed for the better. I felt powerful and in control.

I looked past his shoulder, trying to spot something that would show my reflection. Nothing. That could wait. Right now, I had a nosy person to deal with. I looked straight into his eyes and he backed away. Good. "Miss Clevis had to leave suddenly," I told him. "She was called away."

"Oh dear. I hope she's okay," he said. "I was just speaking with her before lunch."

"She'll be fine. But I was brought in to substitute." I smiled and he took another step back. "Now, if you'll excuse me, I have a class waiting."

I walked away from him. He didn't say anything else. I had the feeling he wanted to hide from me. Good. Fear meant power.

I climbed the steps and headed toward the science class. A whole room full of students were chatting and babbling.

"*Silence!*" I shouted as I walked in through the door.

Every head turned toward me. Good. Fear was in their eyes. I stormed over to the chalkboard and wrote MS. HYDE. "I'm your substitute," I told them.

In the back of the room, a large boy laughed.

"You!" I shouted, pointing at him. "There's nothing

funny going on. There will be no laughing in this class. Do you understand?"

He nodded.

I stared one by one at the students. Each one looked away. None could meet my gaze. Except Dawn. She smiled at me with kindness. How disgusting. I'd have to find a way to remove that smile. She needed to be punished for her cheerfulness.

A hand shot up.

"What?" I asked. It was Norman. But I couldn't call on him by name. I was supposed to be a stranger.

"How long will Miss Clevis be absent?" he asked.

"Do I look like a doctor?" I walked over to him and glared down at his pointy little head. "Do I look like I can predict the future? Is it even any of your business?"

He opened his mouth. I suspect he planned to launch an answer filled with those big words he so dearly loved, but his face grew pale as I glared at him, and nothing came out but a thin gasp that sounded like a tire slowly going flat.

"Now," I said, picking up the book from my desk. "Read chapters eighteen and nineteen. Make sure you finish before the end of the class. You shouldn't have any trouble. It's only thirty pages."

Several of them started to make sounds of protest.

"Silence!" I screamed.

They were silent. Good. I could fill up the whole period this way. It would be better—and more fun—to teach them something wrong or harmful, but for the moment this would do. They would get nothing of value from cramming two chapters into their minds. They'd probably start to hate science. Wonderful.

While they opened their books, I walked to the back of the room. There was a mirror inside the coatroom. I switched on the light and examined my reflection.

I was beautiful. All the softness, all the weak kindness that had marred the face of Miss Clevis was gone. I looked at a face filled with power and control. Marvelous.

Time passed. I could have looked at myself for hours, but there would be plenty of chances for that later. Right now, I had a whole classroom of students under my control, and I was ready to have some fun with the little darlings.

Six

BASHING SEBASTIAN

Where should I start? I wondered as I stormed out of the coatroom. I saw kids straightening up as I walked past. They were all trying so hard to avoid my attention that I could feel their efforts. *Where to start?*

"You!" I shouted, pointing at Sebastian. "Stop talking."

He looked up from his book, a wonderfully shocked expression distorting his face. "I wasn't talking," he said.

"You're talking now," I said. "Aren't you?"

"Yes."

"And you're still talking," I said. "Even though I asked you to stop."

38

"But—"

"Stop talking!" I shouted.

His mouth dropped open. I could tell he was struggling to answer me without talking. Finally, he nodded.

I could have kept on tormenting him for a while longer, but it would be bad manners to ignore the rest of the class. There were so many victims who needed my attention. I spun toward the boy on Sebastian's right. It was wonderful. I could feel the tension grow stronger on the side of the room I was facing. And I could feel the tension grow weaker behind my back. I could ride the stress in the room like an ocean current.

"What are you looking at?" I asked.

"Nothing."

"Stop talking and get back to work."

This was so much fun. I checked the clock. Just five minutes left. Perfect. "Close your books," I told them.

The books snapped shut. "Take out your notebooks. Write everything you remember from the two chapters you just read."

A couple of the braver ones groaned, but I quickly silenced them. They got to work, their faces etched with the wonderfully sad expressions of the doomed. It would be a splendidly hopeless exercise. I was sure most of them hadn't paid much attention to what they were reading. They were all too worried about what I would do next. And they were all too worried about completing an impossible assignment.

What joy. Teaching was such a rewarding profession.

When the bell rang, they filed out, dropping their papers on my desk. They hurried from the room. *Run, you cowards.* None of them dared look me in the eyes. With one sickening exception. Dawn glanced at me. Her face was filled with an expression of pity. It made me want to throw up.

"What are you staring at?" I snapped. "Get out of here."

She rushed from the room.

I sat down to grade the papers. That would be fun. I could just have marked them all with an F. But I wanted to give the grades a little more thought than that. Let's see. Top of the pile—last paper handed in. Bud Mellon. The large boy in the back. He'd never gotten a good grade even once in his life. I decided to give him an A. That would shake him up. He wouldn't have any idea why he'd done so well. Better yet, that would give him false hope so I could crush him even harder the next time.

Okay. Let's just mark a couple with an F, then a couple with a D. I decided to throw in a few more A's, just to get the others jealous. Jealousy is a wonderful way to make kids hate each other. Ah, I reached Norman's paper. An F would kill him. But I smiled as I realized that a C would be even better. Norman almost always got an A-plus. He might have had a rare B or two. But never anything lower. An F was too big a jump. Yes. The C would be perfect.

"Ms. Hyde."

I looked over toward the door. Curses. It was Dawn. "Why are you bothering me? Can't you see I'm grading papers? Would you like to get detention?"

She shook her head. "I just wanted to welcome you to Washington Irving. I'd bet it's hard being a substitute. I just wanted to let you know I'm glad you're here."

She smiled that sickeningly sweet smile of hers, gave a little wave, then raced away like some sort of innocent little forest creature.

Disgusting. I tried to get back to grading, but she'd ruined all the pleasure of that activity, at least for the moment.

I stood up.

Maybe I got up too fast. Another wave of dizziness washed over me, sweeping darkness into my mind.

Seven

TAKE A SEAT

Goodness.

I stood at the desk, puzzled and ashamed. I couldn't believe I'd been so mean and rotten. How could I have treated those wonderful children so nastily? Wait. Who was I? I rushed back to the coatroom and checked the mirror.

I was Jackie. Thank goodness. I studied my face carefully. There was no sign of meanness in my expression. No trace of evil in my eyes. I guess I could even say I was pretty. It's okay to say good things about yourself, if they're true. That's not really bragging. It's just being honest.

But this wasn't the time to think about faces or

mirrors or honesty. I had to get out of the room before the next class came in.

I heard a crackle. Then a voice came from the loudspeaker. It was the school secretary, Mrs. Lake. "Attention, students. It's time for the assembly. Fourth, fifth, and sixth grades are to report to the auditorium now."

That was a break. I could slip out of the school. And do what? I didn't know. But I needed time to think about what was happening to me and to figure out what to do about it.

I stepped into the hall, then went downstairs. As I walked toward the back door, I heard a slow, steady tapping sound from around the corner. It was Mr. Brickner. I didn't want to run into him right now.

I ducked into the auditorium.

"Jackie, over here."

I looked at the back row, where Dawn was waving to me. "Hi," I said when I slipped into a seat. "Thanks."

All around me, I could hear the kids, most of whom had just been in science, talking about the new substitute.

"Unbelievable," Sebastian said. "Did you see what she did to me. She's crazy."

"Inconceivable," Norman said. "Her actions moved beyond the abnormal into the pathological."

"Give her a chance," Dawn said.

They all stared at her.

"You've got to be kidding," Sebastian said. "I'd rather give her a bus ticket to some other planet."

"Sebastian," Norman said, "you know full well a bus is incapable of making an interplanetary journey. Nevertheless, I share your sentiment."

"Maybe she had a reason for being mean," Dawn said. "We don't know where she came from or what's happened to her."

That's for sure, I thought. I didn't want to get involved, but I couldn't help speaking up. "You shouldn't be so hard on her," I said.

Dawn smiled and nodded. Nobody else paid any attention to me. That was okay. I was a stranger. They didn't have any reason to listen to me. I understood.

Sebastian shook his head and told Dawn, "You're such a goody-goody, it makes me sick." He stuck his finger in his mouth and made gagging sounds like he was going to throw up.

The assembly started. A man came up on the stage and talked about how we needed to make the right choices in life. And he did magic tricks. After each trick, he'd explain how it had something to do with an important part of being a good citizen.

"This is pathetic," Sebastian said.

"I like magic," Norman told him. "From a purely scientific standpoint, of course. It's quite an enjoyable sociological phenomenon that merits a great degree of study."

"You're pathetic, too," Sebastian said.

Dawn shushed them.

Sebastian was right, in a way. The magician wasn't very good with his tricks. But he was trying hard to teach us a lesson, and it would have been wrong to criticize him. So I sat and enjoyed the show. There wasn't much else I could do at the moment. I'd never really thought about it before, but kids in school were a captive audience. Whatever assembly the school wanted to have, the students didn't get a choice. This wasn't a bad thing, but it sure made the school's decision an important one.

I realized it made every classroom lesson pretty important, too. If it was a bad or boring lesson, the students were still stuck there. As I watched the magician, I promised that I'd never teach a boring lesson. Then again, if I stayed the way I was, I wouldn't be teaching any kind of lesson at all.

When the assembly ended, I slipped out of the building and went to the parking lot. My car keys were in my pocket. That was good. But as I reached for the car door, I realized I had a problem. I looked like a girl. If I tried to drive, there was a pretty good chance a policeman would stop me. Then what could I do? I don't think any policeman would believe the truth. *Officer, pay no attention to my appearance. I'm really a science teacher who got turned into a girl.* I opened my wallet and looked at my driver's license.

It was an awful photo. But all drivers' license photos are awful. Still, awful or good, it didn't look like me. I studied the picture, then looked at myself in the car mirror. Goodness. I could be my own little sister.

No. I couldn't drive home. I'd have to walk. At least it wasn't all that far—just a mile and a half past the other side of town. That was fine. I liked walking. Behind me, I could hear the dismissal bell. School was getting out. I'd just be another kid in the crowd heading home.

At least, that's what I thought I'd be.

Eight

A GOOD INFLUENCE

I headed toward the center of town. It was a wonderful day—the kind of perfect spring afternoon when the air is just warm enough and the breeze is just gentle enough and the sky is just cloudy enough to make the world seem bright and cheerful. Birds were chirping everywhere, making wonderful music. I stopped walking and closed my eyes, turning my face toward the sunshine.

As I stood there, I was startled by a cry of pain. "Hey, leave me alone."

I opened my eyes and turned toward the shout. A group of sixth-graders was teasing a little kid. He looked like a second- or third-grader. They'd trapped him inside a circle and were blocking his attempts to break free. I could tell he was about to start crying. I couldn't blame him. It was no fun being picked on or bullied. I ran over toward them.

"Leave him alone," I said. As the words left my mouth, I realized I didn't sound like an adult. My voice was the voice of an eleven-year-old girl. I didn't look like an adult, either. There was no reason the boys would pay any attention to me. I didn't have any authority. But what they were doing was mean and wrong, and I had to stop them. Nobody had the right to push anyone else around like that.

The boys looked at me. I knew them from school. They weren't bad kids. They just got in trouble once in a while, probably mostly because they wanted attention. The leader, Joey Sternbacker, stared at me. "What did you say?"

"Please don't tease him," I said. I knew there was no way they'd listen to me. I braced myself for his angry reply.

But as I held his gaze, his glare softened. I could feel him trying to hold on to his meanness. I answered this with a gentle smile.

"Mind your own business," he told me. His tone was less angry, though there was still a slight edge of danger in his voice.

"How'd you like it if someone did that to you?" I asked.

He shrugged, and the tension left the air. It felt like a bomb had been defused. He turned to the others and said, "She's right. We should leave the little kid alone."

The others nodded. Much to my surprise and pleasure, they each apologized to the boy. Then they left.

The boy came up and hugged me. "Thanks," he said.

"Sure." I watched as he ran off, wondering exactly what had happened. It almost seemed like I'd helped the sixth-graders decide to be good instead of bad. But I hadn't done anything. I hadn't really said much. Just a couple words. A smile.

Still, if I could make people act better, that was wonderful. Anything that made the world a better place was good.

"Hey kid, get out of my way!"

I was jerked from my thoughts by the angry words a man was snarling at me. He was walking toward me carrying a bunch of packages.

"Come on. Move!"

I stepped aside. "Sorry," I told him as he rushed past.

He just glared at me.

Wow. I sure hadn't brought out his good side. Maybe I brought out whatever was deep inside people. The man might have had nothing but anger inside himself. Or maybe it was all my imagination. Either way, he'd sure been mean. There was never any excuse for being that rude and nasty.

50

I didn't get a chance to think about it. Another wave of dizziness flooded over me. I felt like I'd just stepped off a very fast carnival ride—like the Tilt-A-Whirl—and couldn't get the ground to stop spinning. I realized I needed to get off my feet before I fell. I spotted a bench by the curb just ahead. I staggered over to it and sat down.

But I wasn't just dizzy. It was worse than that. "Not again," I said as I felt the goodness start to drain out of me. My happiness flowed from my body like water from a shattered aquarium. I tried to fight the change. I tried to hold on to Jackie.

Think good thoughts. I told myself to think about good things. *Sunshine . . . puppies . . . fresh strawberries . . .*

The last thing I wanted was to become that awful Ms. Hyde again.

Nine

FUN IN THE MALL

Broken bones . . . war . . . diseases . . .

Wonderful images of awfulness filled my mind.

What a dreadful place this is.

I got off the stupid bench and looked around. The sun was glaring down on me. How annoying. And those noisy birds were screeching their annoying songs. How awful.

Ahead, on the corner, I heard a man and a woman arguing about something. I walked toward them, drawn by their anger like flies are drawn to a rotting piece of meat. The closer I got, the angrier they sounded. Wonderful. I stood near them as their shouts grew louder and louder. Finally, the woman spun away from the man and ran off.

The sounds of their fight lingered in my brain. I could almost taste the anger. I could almost touch the hurt and rage that lingered in the air. How marvelous. I looked around for more pleasure.

Perfect. A full supply of bad feelings rose ahead of me—Lewington Mall. There would be plenty of unhappiness and anger there. Children fighting with their parents. Parents yelling at their children. Kids teasing other kids. Lots of greed. Lots of envy.

It would be like a vacation for me. Or like a feast.

I walked inside and felt a wonderful wave of miserable emotions wash over me. Heads turned as I went past. People stared at me. I could understand that. I was beautiful. They all wanted to look like me. They wanted to know me. They'd die for a friend like me. Poor, miserable creatures.

The thought of their envy made me laugh. I wandered deeper into the mall, toward the center. On my left, a hardware store had set up a display of paint cans in a pyramid. I yanked out the bottom can as I walked past. The rest tumbled to the floor, making a wonderful clatter. People scattered as the cans rolled in all directions. I glanced back, pleased to see that nobody had stopped to help put the cans back on the table.

Just ahead, I saw a mother with a small boy. He was

howling his head off, crying. She dragged him by one arm and told him how bad he was. The anger was delicious. I moved closer. The boy stared at me. His eyes grew wide and he howled even louder. I grinned at him. His face turned pale from fright. I followed them until they reached an exit.

Now what?

There. I knew those boys. A group of sixth-graders. Joey and his pals. Troublemakers. Perfect. I stayed where I was and watched them, eager to see what they would do. They were hanging out in front of the game store, laughing at anyone who looked different. Smirking and mocking. That was good, but I could get them to do even better. I walked over to them. All eyes turned to me. I leaned toward the leader of the group. His eyes locked with mine.

"Run wild," I whispered. "Be bad. Have fun." For a moment, I held my breath, not sure he would react.

Then he let out a whoop of delight and dashed down the corridor. His friends followed, whooping and screaming. They acted like monsters. Perfect. They'd strike fear into those around them. And then, after they'd spread panic and terror, they'd get in trouble.

What a wonderland the mall was.

I wandered for a while, testing my ability to bring out the worst in people. Some people were easy. They had so much anger inside that they were like overripe fruit, dripping juices at the merest touch, ready to burst forth with a fury that fed my deepest needs.

Others were harder. But nobody was so good inside, so wholesome and pure, that I couldn't dredge out at least some small amount of badness.

Ah, speaking of badness, I caught sight of the perfect pair to suit my purposes—Lud and Bud Mellon, the two meanest kids in the school. They were walking down the corridor toward me.

And what was this? A little boy running toward me from the other direction. Maybe he was here on his own. Or perhaps he was lost. What could be more perfect? Time to feed him to the lions. The thought made me smile. As he ran past me, I glanced around to make sure nobody was watching. Then I stuck my foot out.

He tripped over my foot and went flying. With a high-pitched scream of terror, he tumbled through the air, then crashed into Bud Mellon's legs.

It was so wonderful, I trembled in anticipation.

Bud glanced down at the tangled heap quivering at his feet. Lud glanced down, too. I licked my lips, already tasting the mindless flood of cruelty I had set in motion.

Ten

ON THE OTHER HAND

I watched with anticipation as Bud Mellon bent over and reached down toward the little kid. He extended a hand the size of a bear paw and grabbed the kid by the shoulder. A hand that big could crush anything that got it angry. This was great.

"You okay, little fella?" Bud asked.

"Yeah," Lud said, kneeling down next to the kid. "You all right? You really shouldn't run like that. You could get hurt." He gently wiped a tear from under the kid's eye.

The kid sniffled, then nodded. "I'm okay."

"I got a little brother," Bud said. "I hate it when he gets hurt."

I turned away from the sickening scene, feeling so disgusted with their kindness that I wanted to throw up. Maybe I spun too fast. Everything got fuzzy. I hurried down the hall. That is, I tried to hurry. But I was so dizzy, I couldn't walk straight. I stopped and leaned against a wall.

Goodness.

I felt awful as I thought about all the terrible things I'd just done. There was no excuse for any of it. I glanced over my shoulder. Lud and Bud, each holding one of the little kid's hands, walked with him to the information desk. That was good. They'd help him find his mom.

As soon as I could take a step without feeling dizzy, I hurried back to the hardware store. There were still cans scattered on the floor, though most of them had gotten kicked against the side of the store by people passing by. I knelt and started straightening up the mess I'd made.

The mess I'd made?

Wait. That wasn't right. I hadn't made it. It wasn't me. It wasn't my fault. That evil, mean, and cruel person, Ms. Hyde, had done all the bad things. That wasn't me. I was Jackie.

It didn't matter. Someone had to take responsibility. Even if I hadn't done anything, I'd still want to help whenever I could. It usually takes less time to fix something than to figure out an excuse for not helping out.

Someone knelt next to me. A lady joined in to help pick up the cans. I smiled at her and she smiled back. Then a man passing by with his daughter stopped. Before long, the whole display was back the way it had been. I thanked the other people and moved along, looking for any more signs of Ms. Hyde's damage.

Ahead, I heard the sound of a gang of boys making trouble. I sighed and realized it was something I would have to deal with. I spotted them down the corridor. They'd taken a shopping cart from the market. Two of the kids were jammed in the cart, and Joey was pushing them, running through the mall at full speed. The rest of the gang raced along behind them. The mall had only two guards on duty. The problem was that the mall had five corridors coming out from the center. So it was hard for the guards to see everything that was going on.

The kids must have known neither guard was nearby. Or maybe they just didn't care. But the way they were fooling around, someone would get hurt if I didn't stop them. I moved to the center of the corridor and held out my hand.

"Stop," I shouted. "You'll hurt someone."

They bore down toward me. But I knew they'd stop. I'd gotten them to stop before when they were picking on that little boy. All that had taken was a smile and a few words. I knew I could get them to stop again. They weren't really bad. I wasn't in any danger.

They got closer—close enough so I could see the face of the boy pushing the cart. When I got a good look at his eyes, I froze. There was a wildness in his gaze. It hadn't been there before. *Run wild.* It was almost as if he was under a spell.

I thought about my other self. Ms. Hyde. She'd pumped the boys full of bad ideas and sent them running wild. Joey was out of control. If I'd had time to talk to him, to reason with him, maybe I could have stopped him. But there wasn't any time for talk. There was no way to get him to listen to me.

I didn't stand a chance. It was too late to get out of the way. My eyes squeezed shut as the cart reached me. In my mind, I saw the scientific equations that measured the force of a collision. $F = ma$. Force equals mass times acceleration. Any science teacher could tell you that. The faster something is going or the heavier it is, the more damage it can do.

But I didn't need a science degree to figure out the bottom line: This was going to hurt.

Eleven

HANGING OUT

A force from another direction saved me. I was nearly swept off my feet as someone grabbed my right shoulder and tugged me to the side. I opened my eyes in time to see the cart rattle past, just missing me. The boys raced to the end of the corridor, where they met up face-to-face with one of the mall guards. He pointed to the exit and they slunk off.

"Thanks," I said, turning to Dawn. "I think you just saved me from a bad accident."

She shrugged. "It's nothing. But why were you standing there like that?"

"I thought they'd stop if I asked them to," I said. "I guess I was wrong."

61

Dawn nodded. "I guess." Then she smiled and said, "Listen, I was about to go home. Want to come over and hang out for a while?"

"Sure." It would be a good idea to get out of the mall. It was really nice of her to invite me over, especially since she didn't know me very well at all. But that's the sort of girl Dawn was. The sort who was nice to strangers, and the first person to invite a new kid home. The sort who thought about others and always looked for ways to help. I suspected we had plenty in common.

We left the mall and headed toward her house. It felt nice to get out of there. It was a good place to shop, but it also seemed to bring out the worst in people.

"Thanks again," I said to Dawn as we crossed the street. "You're a good person."

"I guess." She sighed and shook her head.

"What's wrong?" I asked.

"Being good isn't all that much fun sometimes," she said. "People step on you. They take advantage and they make fun. It's tough being good. I wish I had some other label. It's always *Oh, Dawn is so nice*, or *That Dawn is such a good girl*. I get tired of it sometimes. I wish just once I could be bad."

Wow. I'd never seen that side of her before. She'd been in my science class all year. But I'd always seen her as her teacher sees a student. And she was right. That's how I thought of her. Nice Dawn who always smiled. Sweet Dawn, the girl who always behaved.

Good Dawn, who did her homework and never made trouble in class. I had one advantage—I knew it was worth holding on to goodness as you grew up. I remembered some tough years when I was in school, but not counting my current problem, I had a pretty good life. "Listen, it might be rough now," I told her. "But the older you get, the easier it will be."

"How do you know?" she asked.

That was a question I couldn't answer right now. If I told her, she wouldn't believe me. "I just know. Trust me."

"I hope you're right. Hey—we're here." She pointed to the house on the corner. "You aren't afraid of dogs, are you?"

"Nope."

A very friendly collie greeted us in the yard. "That's Newton," she told me. "That's Jackie," she told the dog.

"Pleased to meet you," I said, holding out my hand. Newton offered his paw and we shook.

I followed her inside and down the hall to her room. A tall bookshelf and a dresser lined one wall. There were posters and two framed prints on the other walls. One print was a painting of water lilies. The other was a woman with a baby. I recognized the artists as Claude Monet and Mary Cassatt. Dawn had good taste in paintings. "This is very—" I stopped before I said the word.

"Very what?" she asked.

"Nice."

Dawn laughed. "I guess I can't get away from it, can I?"

I shook my head. "There are worse things to be stuck with." That was sure true. I thought about Ms. Hyde. She was certainly a bad thing to be stuck with.

I noticed a table in the corner with a variety of objects on it. Dawn pointed over to it and said, "That's my project for the science fair. Want to see it?"

"Sure."

"My title is *Vision and Perception*." She laughed. "That sounds like something Norman would say."

I nodded in agreement. "But it's okay to use a big word if that's the right word."

"Yeah." Dawn pointed to one of the things she'd built for her project. "For example, that's called a *zoetrope*. There's no other word for it. At least, I don't think there is. Unless you want to call it a *picture thingy* or a *whatchamacallit*."

"Whatchamacallit's a pretty big word, anyhow," I said. I looked at the zoetrope. Dawn had done a nice job with it. It was a very early version of a moving picture. There was a cylinder with slits. On the inside of the cylinder, she'd put a series of drawings, like from a flip book. There was one drawing between each pair of slits. I bent over and looked through one of the slits, then spun the cylinder. The pictures appeared to animate, showing a chick hatching from an egg.

"Cool," I said.

"Thanks." Dawn picked up something else. "Check this out." She handed it to me. It was a round wood stick with a file card attached to the end. On one side of the card, she'd drawn a bird. I turned it over. On the other side, she'd drawn a cage.

"Put the bird in the cage," she said.

I knew the answer, but I didn't want to spoil her surprise.

"Here. I'll show you." Dawn took the stick back from me and twirled it between her palms. The card spun, showing each side quickly enough that my eyes saw both the bird and the cage. She'd put the bird in the cage.

"That's great," I said.

She showed me the rest of her project.

After that, we sat on her floor and looked through some of Dawn's art books. No question—I was having a nice time. I probably should have been worrying about what had happened to me. However at the moment, there didn't seem to be anything I could do. There was no point ruining a pleasant time by worrying.

But as the shadows crept through the sheer curtains of her bedroom window, I knew that I needed to move along. I couldn't stay there. Sooner or later, she'd ask me questions I wasn't ready to answer. I didn't want to lie to her. I suspected I might not even be capable of lying.

"Thanks for inviting me over," I said as I stood up.

"My pleasure," Dawn said.

"Guess I'd better get going."

"Okay. See you tomorrow?"

I nodded. "I hope so."

Dawn went out the front of her house with me. As I was about to leave, she said, "You know, sometimes I envy the kids who misbehave."

"What do you mean?"

"It must be nice to go through life without trying to do everything the right way. I can't stand being late for anything. It would be so nice to be able to show up an hour late and not feel like I'd done something wrong. Or forget my homework and not worry about it."

I just wanted to hug her and tell her that it would be okay. That it would get easier. And that the world would be a terrible place without people like her. I had a funny feeling that the kids she envied didn't like getting in trouble. They were probably just as unhappy with their actions as she was. I reached out and patted her arm. "Dawn, you can't change the way you are. Not the way you are deep inside."

"Yeah. I guess . . ."

"Thanks again for inviting me over." I headed down the road and walked until I was out of sight. Then I stopped. It was hard to walk when you weren't sure where you were going. I'd thought about going home.

That wouldn't do me any good. There was nothing at home that would change things.

But there was one place I could always go to. One place that had plenty of answers.

Twelve

CHECK THIS OUT

I've loved libraries ever since I was old enough to chew on a book. Okay, chewing books is bad, but I got past that stage pretty quickly and moved on to looking at picture books and then reading chapter books as I grew older, and from there I leaped to novels and big thick science books. Wherever I've lived, I've always made sure it was near a good library. And Lewington certainly had a nice one. It wasn't as big as the library across the river in the capital, but it had a great selection of books, and several very helpful librarians.

So there I went.

Now, where to start? I was pretty sure the problem had something to do with the chemicals I'd accidentally put in my breakfast drink. So maybe it was a chemistry problem. But they'd affected my body. So it might be a medical problem. They'd also affected my mind—perhaps more than anything else. So I decided to start with psychology. I went to that section and found several books on personality changes. I brought them back to the reading section and plunked myself down at a table.

"Are you finished yet?"

I looked across the room. Sebastian was there, hovering behind Norman. Without glancing up from his book, Norman said, "No. Not yet. I need to make sure my project is perfect."

"You may as well give it up," Sebastian said. "I'm going to win. I have the coolest project. Flat-out first place. No contest."

"I'm happy for you," Norman mumbled.

I couldn't help watching them. They were so different on the outside. But inside, I think they had a lot in common. They both had good hearts. Maybe that's why they were such good friends. Norman could get so lost in thought, and Sebastian could get so lost in himself, but they were always there for each other. I hoped they'd stay friends as they got older.

I looked away, but not in time. Sebastian caught me

staring at them. He wandered over. I guess he was bored watching Norman read.

"Hi," he said. "You're Dawn's friend. Right?"

"Right." I smiled at him. He was so cute. If I ever got married and had a son, I'd want him to be like Sebastian. He was far from perfect, but there was just something about him that made me like him.

He picked up his backpack and dropped it on the table. "Wanna see my project for the science fair? It's real cool."

"Sure." I fought to keep my smile from turning into a grin. He seemed so proud of his project. Knowing Sebastian, it could be anything from an assortment of moldy food to clay models of famous monsters. Sebastian was wild about monsters, and managed to work them into almost everything he did.

He unzipped his backpack, then started pulling stuff out. "Here it is," he said after digging through comic books, old test papers, candy wrappers, and a couple baseballs. He placed his project on the table in front of me and said, "Ta dah!"

I looked down. Sunglasses? A piece of thin red wire was taped to one frame of the glasses. The wire ran to a small block of wood that was painted black. A second wire ran to a dirty, worn-out gardening glove. Sunglasses and a glove?

"Very nice," I said.

He stood there as if he expected me to say more.

"Very, very nice." I said. "You obviously put a lot of work into it."

"Don't you know what it is?" he asked. His tone suggested I'd just dropped in for a visit from Mars.

I shook my head. "Sorry. I don't."

"It's a virtual reality system," he told me. He pointed to the glasses. "You see everything through here. And you interact with the world through the glove. Everything is hooked up to a miniature supercomputer. Cool, huh?" He tapped the black block of wood. "Eighty terabytes of memory and a five-hundred-gigahertz processor."

I picked up the glasses and put them on. The room got a bit darker, but nothing else happened. "It doesn't do anything," I said.

"It's a model," Sebastian explained. "It's not supposed to do anything. You know. Like the dinosaur model in the museum. It doesn't do anything. Right?"

"Right."

"There are model cars that just sit on a shelf. And stuff like that. So this is a model of a virtual reality system. Get it?"

I nodded. I really didn't know what to say. I guess he was trying his best, but projects had never been Sebastian's strong point. Still, I had to admire his enthusiasm. And nobody would ever worry about his self-esteem. Sebastian thought very highly of himself.

"Good luck with it," I told him.

"Thanks. I'm glad you're not judging the science fair," he said. "Ms. Clevis will see how cool it is. She's a really good teacher."

Norman wandered over. "Okay. I'm done. We can leave," he told Sebastian. He glanced down at the table and said, "Better pack up your sunglasses."

"They aren't sunglasses," Sebastian said as he stuffed everything into his backpack.

"It's tragic to think of your mom out in the backyard, trying to weed her garden with only one glove while squinting in the bright light of the sun," Norman said. "But I guess we all have to make sacrifices in the name of science."

Sebastian started to walk off, then looked back at me and asked, "You really think it needs more work?"

I shrugged. "It never hurts to try to improve something."

"I guess." He headed out of the library with Norman. On the way, I could hear them squabbling and giving each other a hard time the way only best friends can do.

Okay, I told myself. *Back to work.* I searched through the psychology books without finding anything that would help. Then I tried the medical ones. As I was going through the chemistry books, the librarian came over.

"We're closing up, hon," she said. "Would you like to check anything out?"

"No thanks." I got up from the chair and stretched. Then I looked outside. The library closed at nine. It was dark. And I still had to get home.

Thirteen

HEADING FOR HOME

I left the library by the front exit, then sat on the bottom step. The night was beautiful. The air was cool, but not cold. There was just a little bit of a breeze. A couple stars twinkled in the sky, though clouds were starting to build on the horizon. No point in complaining about being on foot. I stood and started walking.

I went to the edge of town, past all the businesses, and headed along Route 37. It wasn't a big highway, and the first part went past houses, so I had a sidewalk. Then, when the road got farther from town, there was a shoulder for me to walk on. At least there wasn't much traffic. But every time a car came by, I felt myself tense up, wondering whether they'd stop and ask me why I was walking by myself on the road at night.

Walking gave me a good chance to think. Obviously, I had changed in some way. There was a physical change, though it really wasn't all that great. It's not like I'd shrunk eighteen inches or sprouted a third arm. I was younger. But I was still me. There was another change, too. It was hard to know for sure, but I think I'd become nicer. Not that I wasn't already nice. I always thought of myself as a decent person. But I guess everyone does.

Now, I was even nicer. I couldn't really explain it beyond that. It was almost as if everything bad had been removed from me. All the things I knew were bad and didn't want to do or be, but sometimes couldn't help, all of that had been pulled out of me.

I searched my mind and thought of what I'd been through these past hours. There didn't seem to be any sign of envy or hate or greed in my actions. None of the bad stuff. But the thought didn't fill me with pride. It was just something that had happened to me. I couldn't take credit for being this good.

But then there was the other me. I thought about Ms. Hyde and shuddered. In truth, I couldn't remember her very clearly. It was almost as if I'd read about her in a book. Whatever she'd experienced, I wasn't really there at the time. She wasn't me. I wasn't her. But we shared this body. Except, when she had control, I was different. That much I knew. Older. Twisted. Evil. Angry.

Perhaps she was gone for good. I hoped so. I really wanted to get back to being myself. To being Miss Clevis. But if I couldn't do that, I'd rather be Jackie than Ms. Hyde. No question.

I was passing by a stretch of woods. Maybe one more mile to my house. Fifteen or twenty minutes more to walk. Not bad. Then, when I got home, I could figure out what I was going to do tomorrow. Maybe I'd go to sleep and wake up as myself. That would be nice.

I tensed as another car cruised by. Lewington is a small town. And it's a safe one. Still, anyone could be passing through on this road. This car didn't sail past like the others. It slowed, then stopped on the shoulder up ahead.

Fourteen

A GOOD
NIGHT'S SLEEP

It wasn't just any car. It was a police car. The driver got out and shone a flashight at me. I squinted in the light. "Hello," the policman said. "Are you all alone?"

"Yes," I told him.

"You aren't running away from home, are you?" he asked.

I shook my head. "No. I'm walking toward home," I told him. That was certainly the truth. I held my breath, hoping he wouldn't treat me like a runaway and take me to the police station.

He pointed to the car. "Can I give you a ride?"

"I'm almost there," I said. "And it's a nice night for walking."

He nodded. "It's a beautiful night. But there are some dangerous people in this world. It would be a shame if you ran into one of them. How about letting me give you a lift?"

I nodded. It was his job. If I didn't take the ride, he'd be worried about me. The best thing I could do was let him help me. That way, everybody won.

"It's just ahead," I told him as we pulled back onto the road. "Third house on the right after the stop sign at the top of the hill."

He nodded. A couple minutes later, he pulled into my driveway. "Here you go. You be careful where you walk. Okay?"

"I will. Thanks." I got out of the car. The policmean waited until I was inside the house. Then he drove away. I watched from the window as the car backed out of the driveway and thought about how tough his job must be. He had to deal with every kind of bad thing that came along, but it hadn't turned him mean. He could still be nice to a young lady walking home on a lonely highway.

I sighed and kicked off my shoes. It felt good to be home. True, I had a big problem to figure out. But at least I was home.

As I was getting ready for bed, I studied myself in the bathroom mirror. I had the face of a sweet young girl, a mostly familiar face. I went to the closet in my bedroom and dragged out a box of old photographs. It took a while, but finally I found one from sixth grade and brought it back to the bathroom. I propped it up against the mirror, then compared it to my reflection. Similar. The girl I saw in the mirror and the girl in the photo could have been sisters. But not twins. I hadn't just become the girl I'd once been.

"Let's be scientific about this," I said. I tried to analyze the situation. But to be honest, I didn't really feel very scientific. Mostly, I felt sleepy.

So I went to bed. As much as I needed sleep, I wish I'd stayed awake. I wish I'd avoided the dreams.

Fifteen

BAD DREAMS

The place was beautiful. It looked like the sort of fairy-tale world you see in cartoon ads for toys or breakfast cereals. There were millions of flowers in a huge meadow, and a sunny sky dappled with fluffy clouds. Rainbow-colored birds swooped and soared while whistling enchanting songs. In the far distance, I saw a gleaming silver castle.

I heard footsteps. A woman was walking ahead of me, moving slowly through the flowers. I ran to catch up with her. I tapped her on the shoulder and she stopped walking, but she kept her back to me. "I think I'm lost," I said. "Can you help me?"

She turned and stared at me with sad eyes. A shiver

ran through me from my scalp to the tips of my fingers. She was me. But me as I'd been before all this started. It was me as Miss Clevis. "I can't stay here," she said.

"Why not?" I asked.

"I don't belong here. If I stay here, I'll lose myself."

I didn't understand. Before I could ask her what she meant, the whole world shook with a giant explosion. Lightning flashed. In an instant, the sky turned dark with heavy clouds. Around me, the flowers died. Thorn-filled vines thrust through the soil, tangling with everything. The birds turned to vultures and began attacking one another. The castle crumbled to the ground and burst into flames.

The place felt so awful, so deep-down bad, that I couldn't help crying. I reached out to grab the woman.

She put an arm around me. "I can't stay in this dark world, either," she said. "This place will destroy me. And not just me."

She was right. I knew it would destroy me, too. It would eat away at me until there was nothing left. I looked for a way out.

There was another crash of thunder. The beautiful world returned. But not for long. With a crash, the bad world was back. It didn't stop. All I wanted was for the world to stay still, but the thunder wouldn't leave me alone. Crash after crash echoed through my head, faster and faster. The worlds flipped back and forth so rapidly that reality spun inside my head.

I screamed and sat up in bed.

Outside, lightning flashed and a clap of thunder shook the house. I gasped for breath. Sweat rolled from my face. "I'm safe," I said, looking around at the room as each flash illuminated it. "This is my home. This is real. That was a dream. Just a dream."

But I realized it was much more than a dream. It was my mind's way of telling me a truth I'd been avoiding all day. A truth I'd hidden from since the reality of the change first hit me.

Right now, I was the good me. I was Jackie. A person with no evil in her. There was also the bad me. Ms. Hyde. A person with no good in her at all. But then, caught in between, was the real me. The me I was. The me I'd been born to be. Not all good. Not all bad. Just all human.

And that me—the real me—was in danger of disappearing. Whether I remained as Jackie or Ms. Hyde, the result would be the same: Miss Clevis would vanish. She'd be gone forever.

I couldn't let that happen.

Sixteen

OFF SCHEDULE

I didn't get much sleep the rest of the night. I was afraid I'd dream again. And my mind was heavy with what I'd learned. The worst part was that I had no idea how to help myself. It was a science problem. But I didn't seem to be able to think clearly about science. Maybe that was one of the parts that I'd lose forever if I stayed as I was. Maybe I was already losing it. Yesterday, the formula for force had flashed through my mind when I almost got hit by the cart. I tried to remember it now. It came, finally, but I had to work to bring it back.

Right now, there was nothing I could do about that.

At least, being up so early, I had plenty of time to walk to school. I really wasn't even sure why I was going back to the school. But I didn't know what else to do. And ever since I'd started teaching at Washington Irving Elementary, the school had been my second home. The other teachers had been my family. I guess the students had almost been like my children.

Teaching was definitely more than just a job for me—it was my life. But right now, I couldn't even do that. *Things will work out,* I told myself. Somehow, they had to.

By the time I reached the front walkway, a large group of kids had arrived. It felt funny walking through the crowd. I recognized most of them as my students, but they didn't recognize me as their teacher. I almost felt like I was watching a movie.

"Jackie. Hi."

I turned to see Dawn, who was standing with two other sixth-grade girls. "Hi."

"Where's your first class?" she asked. "Maybe we have the same schedule. Wouldn't that be great?"

First class? Uh-oh. I hadn't even thought about classes. I didn't have a schedule—worse, I wasn't even registered as a student. I shrugged. "I don't know where I'm going." That was sure true.

"Then you'd better go to the office," Dawn said. "They can give you your schedule."

"Good idea. Thanks." I headed into the building. Now I had a problem. I couldn't go into the office and tell them I was a new student. That wasn't true. But I couldn't just show up in a class, either. The teacher would want to know who I was. If I didn't go to classes, they'd start asking questions, too. Someone would want to know why I was wandering around in the halls all day.

I stood outside the office, wondering what to do. The bell rang. The hall filled with students heading for their first class. Still, I stood at the door. The crowds thinned. The last few stragglers went to their rooms.

Taking a deep breath, I reached for the doorknob. But I still didn't know what I was going to do. I was so caught up in my thoughts that the quiet tapping sound didn't get my attention until it was too late.

Whack! The tip of the cane smacked the wall next to the door. "You! Why are you standing around? Don't you have a class to go to?"

I spun toward Mr. Brickner. "I—"

"Don't give me any lip. You kids always have an excuse. Well, I don't want to hear it. Understand? Get going! Now!"

I nodded and dashed down the hall. As I reached the corner and stumbled out of his view, the first wave of dizziness washed over me.

I knew what was about to happen. Worse, I knew

there was nothing I could do to prevent it. I tried to hold on to good thoughts, but there weren't any. There was nothing but a fuzzy thickness, as if my mind had been wrapped in heavy blankets of wool.

Seventeen

TROUBLE THAT'S HARD TO STOMACH

The memory of that wretched nice girl clung to my mind as I emerged from the dizziness that clouded my thoughts. But she was gone. Hopefully, for good. There were only dim memories of that time when I was Jackie, but even those vague images caused me to shudder. She'd been so sickeningly nice. So hideously sweet and kind. Disgusting.

Maybe it was all my imagination. I couldn't possibly have been that nauseating creature. Nobody that sweet could survive in this world. She'd be destroyed right away. It didn't matter. I was me, and I was feeling powerful. Best of all, I had a free period before my first class. Plenty of time for fun. To other people, this might be a school. To me, it was a playground.

I heard the sound of little feet echoing down the hallway. Perfect. A second-grade boy was hurrying my way. I met up with him in front of the bathroom.

"Where are you going?" I asked.

He pointed at the bathroom door. "My tummy hurts," he said. But it sounded like, *My tummy huts.*

"It huts?" I asked. "What does that mean?"

"It huts!" he said, as if I could understand him better if he got louder. "It huts bad."

"Are you trying to tell me that your tummy hurts?" I asked.

He nodded, his large eyes staring up at me in a plea for sympathy.

"Your tummy?" I asked.

He nodded again, and some of the tension left his face. I guess he was relieved that I understood his problem. Time to show him how wrong he was. "What kind of a stupid word is that?" I screamed at him. "Tummy? What are you? A baby?"

His face flashed between fright and tears, two of my favorite expressions. "My tummy . . . my stomach huts."

I patted him on the head. "Poor boy. Does it hurt bad?" I asked, speaking as tenderly as I could.

"Yeah."

"Real bad?" I asked.

"Yeah. Real bad."

"Don't worry," I told him. I leaned forward and whispered in his ear. "It's probably just your appendix getting ready to burst."

A delicious wave of fear shot from him. At that instant, I realized something wonderful. The more fear and anguish and terror I could produce, the stronger I'd become. And the stronger I became, the harder it would be for anything to make me change. I laughed and left the boy. He was too easy. I needed more of a challenge. That wouldn't be a problem. This place was crammed with opportunities for sorrow.

"Miss, excuse me."

I looked over my shoulder. It was that pathetic Mr. Rubinitski, sticking his head out of his classroom. He waved a hand, gesturing for me to come over. I decided to treat him to the pleasure of my company.

"You're substituting for Miss Clevis, aren't you?" he asked when I stepped over to him.

"Yes."

"You wouldn't happen to know why she's out, would you?" he asked.

Perfect. I could see it in his eyes. He had a crush on her. This was wonderful. "I believe she ran off to get married," I said.

He opened his mouth. At first, all that came out was a tiny gulp, like a frog might make if you squeezed it hard enough. Then he managed to gasp out the word, "Married?"

I nodded. "Rich fellow. He swept her right off her feet. I believe they're taking his private jet to Hawaii. She's probably not coming back to school." I smiled sweetly at him.

He slumped back into his classroom, looking like a man whose whole world had collapsed around him. I realized his pain made me feel wonderful. This had been even better than scaring the little boy. Terror was tasty, but heartbreak offered special rewards. And I'd ruined all his hopes without raising my voice. Variety was certainly the spice of life.

The best was yet to come. The bell rang. Unlike the rest of the week, on Fridays I had my sixth-grade science class during second period. Norman and Sebastian and the whole gang. All mine. Time for me to devour a roomful of waiting victims. The very thought made me shiver with joy.

Eighteen

DOWN IN THE DUMPS

I hurried to the room so I could watch each one of them walk in. It was lovely the way they squirmed when they noticed me and exchanged glances with one another. Several of the bolder ones dared a whispered word or two among themselves.

Fabulous. I'm sure they'd been hoping to get their precious Miss Clevis back. I guess my presence disappointed them. Perfect. Except for one problem: Dawn. Curse her. She smiled at me. How dare she be so cheerful? It almost made me throw up. For a moment, I braced myself against a slight dizziness, but I looked away from her, and the feeling left. I'd have to change her attitude. Fast.

There was no reason not to have some fun with her. I picked up a notepad and wrote: *Please ask Principal Wardner to explain to this girl the importance of honesty.* That was certainly a marvelously vague request. Then I folded the paper and walked over to Dawn's desk. I dropped the note in front of her and said, "Would you be so kind as to take this to the secretary for me? Wait for an answer."

"Sure. I'd be happy to," Dawn said, giving me another sickening smile. I grinned back at her and stepped away, holding on to the wonderful thoughts of what would happen when she gave the secretary the note. She'd end up getting a lecture from the principal, and she'd probably have no idea what she'd done wrong. He'd start talking to her about honesty, and he'd think she'd been dishonest. And she wouldn't have a clue why she was getting a lecture. Best of all, she was so disgustingly honest that she'd never think of reading the note before she got to the office.

Sometimes I amazed myself. But there was no time to stand around congratulating myself on my cleverness— I had a class to destruct. I mean, instruct.

I studied the students carefully as I planned my next move. Their faces reminded me of mice in a tiger's cage. If I'd shouted, *Boo!* they would have leaped straight off their seats. But that was too easy. It was always better to strike with the unexpected. "Hello, class," I said, using my sweetest voice.

Nobody answered.

"Hello, class," I said again, sounding hurt.

A couple of them said hi. Then a couple more.

"I have your tests graded," I told them. I walked from desk to desk, handing back the test papers, enjoying each expression of shock or surprise.

Norman didn't react at all when I first gave him his test. I walked down the aisle, wondering how long it would take for the shock to wear off.

It took about half a minute.

"You gave me a C?" Norman finally shouted, leaping up from his seat and thrusting out the paper in a clenched fist.

"If you need extra help, I'll be happy to stay after class with you," I told him. "I realize science can be difficult."

"But . . ." He sputtered for a moment or two, but didn't seem to be able to launch his usual string of words. Wonderful. Things got even better when I handed Sebastian his test.

"Hey, Norman," Sebastian said, holding up the paper. "Check it out. I aced the exam. Great, huh?" He grinned at his friend. "Man, I was sure I'd flunked. This is awesome." It was amazing how unaware he was of Norman's feelings. I loved it.

The sound of a garbage truck caught my attention. As I glanced out the window into the parking lot, a brilliant idea hit me. "Come on, class," I said. "Follow me. It's time for our field trip." I led them out to the parking lot and went to my car.

"Pile in," I said, flinging open the door of the Volkswagen.

"But that's Miss Clevis's car," someone said.

"She let me borrow it," I explained, dangling the keys I'd pulled from my pocket.

"We can't all fit," Sebastian said.

I grinned at him. "Aren't you clever to notice that. But it's not a problem." I pointed across the field to the Dumpster that had just been emptied by the garbage truck. "Roll that over here," I said. I pointed back to Sebastian. "Get me some rope from the supply closet."

It was wonderful how quickly they followed my orders. When Sebastian brought the rope, I tied the Dumpster to the rear bumper of my car. "Okay. Hop in."

There were some protests, but they all got in. I started up the car and headed out to the local landfill. It was on the other side of Anderson Swamp, and a long stretch of the road was flooded with an inch or two of muddy water. All the better.

I took the curviest roads I could. The Dumpster swung on the rope, throwing the kids from side to side. It was marvelous.

I could hear them yelping and shouting through my open window.

Norman found his lost vocabulary again and kept

up a running commentary. "Fascinating. Note the effect of angular momentum. Observe the interaction of acceleration and inertia. Notice how—whooooops—!" he screamed as I drove full speed around a tight curve.

Sebastian started shouting when he discovered a couple bugs crawling around in the Dumpster. I'd have to make sure to introduce him to plenty more bugs when I got the chance. I hit a bump in the road, sending the Dumpster into the air. It landed with a jolt. What fun.

"We're here," I said when I pulled up near a towering pile of garbage. I'd driven all the way around to the back of the dump. "Better take off your shoes so you don't get them dirty. Toss them in the car so they won't get lost."

It's amazing what kids will do when a teacher asks them. After I'd gotten all the shoes, I hopped in the car and drove off. Lovely. It was about ten miles back to town, assuming you cut straight across the dump. It was a lot longer if you went around. There wasn't a phone between here and there, and students weren't allowed to bring their own phones to class. *Have a nice walk,* I thought as I headed back to the school. I put the Dumpster where it belonged, then went to the office.

"I need to report some truants," I told the secretary in the office.

"Really?" she asked. "Who?"

"My whole class," I said. "They didn't show up. I

suspect it's some kind of prank. You know—take advantage of the substitute." I stopped to sniffle a bit.

The secretary ran around the desk and put a hand on my shoulder. "There, there. Don't let it get to you. Kids can be cruel sometimes. But I'm sure they didn't mean to hurt your feelings."

I nodded and sniffled some more. "Thank you. You're very kind." I felt a flicker of dizziness, but not enough to worry me. I looked past her into the principal's office. Dawn was there, getting a lecture. I grinned at her. I held my breath as she caught sight of me, bracing for a smile. But she glared back. Excellent. A victory for my side. Even cheerful girls had their limits. It felt especially wonderful to wipe away her smile. There was something about her that worried me. Something about her happy attitude that made me extremely uncomfortable.

But that wouldn't be a problem anymore. She'd gotten a good taste of unfairness. That was almost always guaranteed to turn a person bitter. And, to me, nothing tasted sweeter than bitter.

I spent the rest of the day enjoying my classes. Not that my classes enjoyed me. No, they sure didn't get anything to smile about. For starters, I pulled out all the smelliest chemicals I could find. Pretty soon, the room stank worse than the back end of a sick cow. I gave them tests they couldn't possibly pass. I screamed and yelled. Just when they were getting used to my anger, I smiled and praised them. Teaching certainly was turning out to be a satisfying occupation.

Then, as the day ended and I was leaving the building, I caught sight of one more perfect victim. The day had been dinner. Now, it was time for dessert. There he was. A little boy—just a kindergartner, walking down the hall by himself.

A million wonderful possibilities flooded my mind as I stalked him. I felt just like a spider. A huge, hungry spider.

Nineteen

A GIFT FOR KINDNESS

I'd have to wait until I saw his face before I'd know the best way to torment him. But that was all part of the fun. I sneaked up on him from behind, then suddenly shouted, "Young man!"

He spun toward me. Ah. Sebastian's brother. I smiled, thinking about how Sebastian and the rest of the class were still walking back to school. Walking barefoot through garbage and swamp water, hiking across ten miles of roads.

Rory looked up at me with those big kindergarten eyes. He smiled, then reached in his backpack and held up an apple in his hand. "I saved this from my lunch for you."

I stared at the apple. "What for?" I snapped, trying to take control of the situation.

"Teachers get apples all the time. But substitutes don't. At least, I guess they don't. So I didn't want you to feel left out. So here." He thrust the apple right up at my face.

I took a step away from him.

"Go on. Take it," he said.

I turned and ran down the hall, unable to bear his disgusting kindness. Didn't he know that kids his age weren't supposed to think about anyone but themselves? What was wrong with him? Dizziness crashed against me. That wretched, awful feeling . . .

My goodness.

I was far down the hall and around the corner before I stopped running. The memories of the day ripped at me. I shuddered, trying to fling the images of Ms. Hyde from my mind. Finally, as the last of the dizziness left, I settled down. I turned and rushed back to find Rory. He was probably disappointed that his gift had been rejected.

"Hi," I said. "Ms. Hyde forgot her apple."

Rory nodded. "Maybe she doesn't like them."

I shook my head. "No. I think she was in a hurry. It was very nice of you to do that for her. You're a really sweet kid."

He held up the apple. "Want it?"

"Sure. Thank you very much." I took the apple

from him. What a great kid. As he left, I thought about all the other kids Ms. Hyde had tormented today. There was nothing I could do about the past. But at least I could control the present.

Thinking about the last two days, I understood more of what had been happening to me. There was a pattern. The change from Jackie to Ms. Hyde wasn't random. Any type of goodness—any great act of kindness—could pull me from my evil side. Rory's actions had done it. So had Dawn's kindness earlier. And Lud's actions in the mall.

But it worked both ways: Bad acts drove Jackie away, leaving the door open for Ms. Hyde to return. I knew that if I wanted to keep from becoming Ms. Hyde again, I'd have to stay away from anger and hatred and anything else that came from the dark side of human nature.

That would be difficult. Maybe even impossible. But I had to try. I had to stay as Jackie if I ever wanted to become Miss Clevis again. As Jackie, I could search for a cure. Ms. Hyde would never want a cure. She'd want to stay as she was.

And each time I became her, she got stronger. Worse, she drove the goodness out of all those around her. Look what she'd done to Dawn. Sooner or later, she'd try to destroy Rory.

Poor Dawn. I realized she must have been hurt by

all she'd gone through. I had to see her and try to fix the damage that Ms. Hyde had done.

I just hoped she wasn't so filled with anger that she drove me back to being Ms. Hyde. It was a chance I'd have to take.

Twenty

FACE-TO-FACE

I found her sitting on her front porch, brushing Newton. Even from a distance, I could tell she was still hurt and angry. This could be dangerous. If she lashed out with her bitterness, I might get flung back into being Ms. Hyde. And that wouldn't just be bad for me. I knew that Ms. Hyde would do whatever she could to destroy Dawn, or to drag her down to that world where everything was anger and hate. And an angry Dawn would have no chance against whatever other attacks Ms. Hyde launched.

"What a beautiful dog," I said.

Dawn looked up from the dog. "Oh, hi." No smile.

I hesitated for a moment. But a thought gave me

courage: If Ms. Hyde could bring out the bad side of people, maybe I could bring out the good side. And with Dawn, there was already so much goodness. I walked over to the bottom of the porch steps.

"What's the matter?" I asked. "You look upset."

"That awful teacher," Dawn said, glaring at me. "She got me in trouble. And I didn't do anything." She threw down the dog brush. "It's not fair."

This wasn't going well. I could feel her anger. It splashed over me like acid. I took a step back. What could I tell her? That life was fair? No. That wasn't true. Sometimes life wasn't fair. Good things happened to bad people. And bad things happened to good people.

"Not fair at all," she said.

I couldn't lie to her. But I couldn't walk away. And if I stayed, I was sure the waves of hate and self-pity would push me back to where I didn't want to go. There was only one thing I could do.

"Hey, I'm really sorry you feel bad," I said, taking a step back toward her. "You're a good person. It hurts me to see you unhappy."

She looked right into my eyes. I could almost see her own good and bad sides waging war. Newton lifted his head and licked Dawn's cheek.

"See," I said. "He's sorry, too."

She smiled. It was as if a light had been switched on in a dark cave. "Thanks. It's been a rough day."

"You're telling me." I smiled back.

Dawn patted the porch next to her. I climbed the steps and sat down. Newton acknowledged my presence by rolling on his back and letting me rub his belly.

"Where'd he get his name?" I asked.

"From the scientist," she said.

"Do you like science?" I asked.

Dawn nodded. "I don't get the greatest grades in the world, but I really like science. We've got a really good science teacher, too."

"That's great," I said, interrupting her. I didn't want to hear praise about myself when she didn't know that I was me. It wouldn't be right.

"If there's one thing Miss Clevis taught us, it's to make careful observations. And to look for connections." Dawn stopped talking and stared at me.

I glanced down at the steps. "So what have you observed?" I asked.

"Miss Clevis, who's never been sick as far as I can remember, is suddenly gone. At the same time, two new people show up." She paused again as if she suddenly realized another connection. Then she gasped. "And I've never seen those two together."

"You never will," I told her.

"Jackie," she asked, "what's really going on? Who are you?"

Twenty-one

TELLING THE TALE

"This might be a little hard to believe," I said. It was still hard for me to believe, and I'd been living through it.

"I'll believe you," she said. "Just tell me."

So I told her what I knew. I explained about the changes. And about the evil side of me. "Anything bad could make me change back," I said. "Please, be real careful not to get angry around me."

"Don't worry," Dawn told me. "I'll be careful. I don't get angry much, anyhow. I wouldn't even be angry today if it wasn't for that whole stupid thing in the principal's office. I couldn't believe he gave me that lecture. I didn't do anything to deserve it. It's not—"
She stopped and clamped a hand over her own mouth.

"I'm okay," I assured her. But even that small burst of anger had hurt me.

She lowered her hand. "Sorry."

"Don't worry about it."

"Hey—if you're aware of Ms. Hyde, do you think she's aware of you?"

That was a good question. "As far as I can remember, she thinks differently. I can accept that I have a bad side. But I don't think she can truly accept that she has a good side. She's too proud to see herself as she really is."

Dawn sat for a while. So did I. It was nice being on the porch with her and her dog. It didn't solve anything, but it was a good place to be. Finally, she spoke three words that went right to the center of the problem: "So now what?"

"I have to figure out how to become myself again. There has to be a way. If I can be forced to become Ms. Hyde or Jackie, maybe I can be forced back to being Miss Clevis. I just don't know how."

"But you're a science teacher," Dawn said. "You have to figure something out. Look at all the stuff you taught me. Think about the science fair. All those kids learned what they know from you. My project's not great—but it wouldn't be even half as good if you weren't my teacher."

"But I'm not me right now," I said. "I mean, I'm not the science teacher." I guess there was still a science teacher deep inside of me, because I had an idea. I thought about the fair. And about Dawn's project. "Let's go up to your room," I said. Maybe there was an answer. . . .

Before we could move, Newton picked his head up from Dawn's lap and looked down the street. I looked, too. Sebastian and Norman were heading our way, walking down the sidewalk in their bare feet. Their pants legs were all wet and muddy, and their shirts were drenched with sweat.

Newton barked. Sebastian and Norman looked over.

"Wow," Dawn said, calling to them. "You sure look like a mess. What happened?"

"What happened?" Sebastian yelled. "I'll tell you what happened!" His anger washed over me.

Twenty-two

HOW TO DRIVE
SOMEONE ANGRY

"That stupid, ugly, idiotic substitute. That's what's the matter." Sebastian kicked the bottom step of the porch. "I hate her!"

"Sebastian, stop!" Dawn shouted. "You're angry."

"Of course I'm angry, you twit!" he yelled. "You'd be angry too if you'd just spent the day walking barefoot through a dump, a swamp, and a road where every single person in town must have taken their dogs for a walk. Horses, too, from what I could tell. You think a dump is bad? At least most of the stuff is in bags. Do you have any idea what kind of trash people throw out on the road?" He kicked the step again.

"This was unconscionable behavior," Norman said. "I'm virtually inarticulate with rage!"

I stood up and staggered down the steps, searching around for a way to escape.

"Just shut up, okay?" Dawn said, her own voice tinged with anger. "You're making trouble."

"I'm making trouble?" Sebastian said. "Me? Who are you to talk? You got to run some errand to the principal's office and miss out on the whole wonderful field trip. Teacher's pet. You had it easy."

"Easy?" Dawn said. "You jerk."

The rest was just an angry buzz. I pushed between Norman and Sebastian and raced toward the sidewalk, trying to get away from them before the change took hold of me.

"Wait!" Dawn called. "I'm sorry. We didn't mean to be angry."

At the corner, I spun back to face them. The world turned dark in an instant. Then everything got clear. Little monsters. That's what they were. I'd take care of them. All of them. And the little brother, too. I'd show them fear and anger. But not yet. Right now, I needed time to plan. I needed time to gather my strength. But that wouldn't be hard. Lewington lay ahead of me, ripe with opportunities, filled with chances to drive people to the depths of misery.

I ran back to the school and got my car. What better way to cause chaos? I roared out of the parking lot entrance, right in front of a delivery truck, forcing the driver to jam on his brakes. The shriek of tires was like a song to me. At the next corner, I got right up behind a woman at the light and honked my horn. She turned and glared at me. I laughed and waved at her. Then I slowed down to a crawl, so the traffic piled up behind me.

For the next hour, I made as many people as I could furious. The thought of all that anger thrilled me. Better yet, I knew each angry person would take that anger and spread it to everyone he met. The truck driver I'd cut off would cut someone else off. The woman I'd honked at would honk at someone else. I'd thrown a rock in a pool, spreading a ripple of rage that went on and on.

As wonderful as the car was for making the world a miserable place, I started to grow tired of it. I needed a change. I needed to do something splendidly awful. Instead of ruining one person's day at a time, I wanted to make the whole town miserable.

I drove home. All night, I thought about the best way to make Lewington suffer. Even in my sleep, I dreamed of schemes. When I woke, it all fell together. What a perfect plan.

I knew just where to go.

Twenty-three

A DANGEROUS
REACTION

As soon as I got dressed, I hurried out of the house.
There wasn't much time.

The lock on the side door to the school had been
broken years ago. Nobody ever worried about it, because Lewington is such a nice, safe place. Fools. I
slipped inside the building and headed to the gym.
Everything was set up for the science fair. I guess other
teachers had stepped in to help during Miss Clevis's
absence. I looked around, searching for the best way to
turn the event into a total disaster.

At first, I didn't see anything promising. There's
little chance for disaster in the typical science fair project. Most of them are just made up of wood or wire or

papier-mâché. Nothing dangerous. But thanks to one student, this wasn't a typical science fair. And there it was, the answer to my hopes, sprawling across the top of four card tables—Norman's scale-model nuclear reactor. Thank goodness he had so much brilliance and so little common sense. What a marvelous combination.

I went over and examined it. As far as I could tell, it was just like a full-sized reactor. He'd even made up a set of miniature instruction books and a thin book with a bright red cover labeled DISASTER EVACUATION PLAN. How charming.

And how appropriate for my plans.

If the cooling cycle failed, the reactor would overheat. Then it would melt down and turn the gym into a radioactive mess. Nobody would be able to go near the school for a couple hundred thousand years. That would certainly ruin a lot of things for a lot of people. Of course, that would happen only if the cooling system failed. And of course, I was going to make sure that it would do just that.

It took me less than ten minutes to find the thermostat and move the probe outside the reactor core. Perfect. Now, no matter how hot it got, the reactor would act like it wasn't overheating.

I slipped back in my car and sat in the driver's seat so when people started to arrive in the parking lot, it would look like I'd just gotten there myself. Pretty soon, they opened up the school. Students and teachers started to show up, along with lots of parents. The more, the better.

Norman was one of the first ones there. He ran inside. I knew where he was headed. He wanted to start up his reactor, so it would be running at full power by the time the fair got under way. It would be at full power, all right. I checked my watch. It was nine thirty. The fair started at ten. In a couple minutes, I'd go inside so I could watch the panic when the reactor started to melt. Then I'd get out before the radiation escaped.

Sebastian showed up, along with Rory. They went in the front with the rest of the crowd. Rory was holding his big brother's hand. It was so sweet, it made me sick.

But there was no sign yet of the one person I really wanted to destroy. Finally, I saw her. Dawn. She was walking toward the school. But she didn't go inside. She went around toward the back of the building. She was carrying something in one hand, but I couldn't tell what it was. Not that it mattered.

This was too perfect. I headed after her. I didn't know what I was going to do, but I knew I was going to make sure she lost her smile. I was feeling powerful. The very thought of the evil I planned gave me enough strength to face her, no matter how happy and cheerful she might be. An old expression came to mind: *I'll wipe that smile off your face.* How true.

Twenty-four

CAUGHT LIKE A RAT

Dawn was standing with her back to me, near the Dumpster. I knew the best approach was a straight-out attack. If I started shouting at her, she'd get angry enough to shout back, especially if I caught her by surprise. It would be lovely.

I took a deep breath, then let her have it. "You! I've had enough trouble with you. Go to the office immediately." That should do it.

She flinched at the sound of my voice, then spun to face me. I couldn't wait to see the look of terror on her face. I knew the memory of it alone would be enough to satisfy me for hours.

"Oh, hello," she said. She held out her hand, offering me a bouquet of flowers. "These are for you."

"*No!*" I shouted, taking a step away from her. Dizziness flicked at the edges of my mind, but I fought it off. "It won't work," I told her. I was stronger than ever and able to fight off her pathetic attack.

"I love you," Dawn said.

Her words struck like a slap to my face. I staggered, but I didn't give up. "I hate you," I snarled back. She flinched. I could feel her losing her control. Time to unleash a stream of words that would crush her completely.

As I opened my mouth, there was a sudden motion behind her. Three faces popped up from inside the Dumpster—Norman, Sebastian, and Rory. "We love you, too," they said.

Too much. The dizziness hit me with the force of a falling tree.

Goodness.

I looked up from the ground. "Did I faint?" I asked.

"Sort of," Dawn said. "You kind of crumpled. But you're okay now."

"Thanks." I still felt weak. I looked at the three kids climbing out of the Dumpster. "And thank you," I said.

"You're welcome," Norman said. "It was Dawn's idea. But she figured she might need some help. We went in the front so you wouldn't get suspicious, then went right out the rear door."

"Yeah," Dawn said. "I was pretty sure you'd follow me back here. But I didn't know if I could be good enough to make you change all by myself. So I asked them to come along." She paused and shook her head. "The funny thing is, when I told them about you, they believed me right away."

"We've seen a lot of strange things in this town," Sebastian said.

"Tons," Rory added.

Wow. They'd really come through for me. They'd kept me from hurting Dawn and they'd changed me back to Jackie. But they hadn't solved my problem. I was still in danger of becoming Hyde at any instant. "We have to try something," I said.

"The bird in the cage?" Dawn asked.

"Yeah." I guess she'd figured out what I'd started to tell her at the porch.

"What bird?" Sebastian asked. "What cage?"

I explained to him about Dawn's illusion with the picture on the stick. "When you see both sides fast enough, they blend into one image. So, maybe if I can change back and forth fast enough, I might end up being both at once. And if I'm lucky, that will make me Miss Clevis again."

"Fascinating hypothesis," Norman said. "And subject to immediate verification."

"What?" Sebastian asked.

"We can try it right now," Dawn said. "We just

122

have to be mean to her until she changes to Ms. Hyde. And then, the second she changes, be nice again."

"What if it doesn't work?" Sebastian asked.

"Then we'd better hope we end up with Jackie," Dawn said, "because if we end up with Ms. Hyde, we're going to be real sorry."

"Ready?" I asked.

Twenty-five

REACTORS

They stood around me in a half circle. "You're all going to have to be as mean as you can," Dawn said. "And then as nice as you can."

"I'm not sure I can be mean," Sebastian said.

"Trust me," Dawn told him. "You can be mean."

"Thanks a lot. I'm not sure I can be nice, either," he said.

"Look. We've all got both inside us," Norman said. "Just do your best."

"Yes," I said. "Just try your best. And whatever happens, thanks for helping me."

The four of them, who'd just rescued me, opened their mouths and let me have it. They called me names and made fun of me. It was shocking hearing such bitter, angry words from such nice people. In an instant, the dizziness came.

Curses.

Where was I? Why were these little monsters talking to me? Those awful smiles. I wanted to smash them all. All that sickening talk about love. What awful beasts they were. I wanted to . . .

Goodness.

I must have fallen again. Why were they shouting? They're so mean. Such angry faces. I could cry. How could they say such terrible things about me?

Drat!

Disgusting animals. That's what they were. Those smiles.

Wonderful smiles.

I hated them.

I . . .

Silence. They stood staring at me. I wanted to hug them. And I wanted to kick myself for getting into this mess. I was happy. And I was angry. Both at once! That meant I couldn't be Jackie. And I couldn't be Ms. Hyde.

"It worked," I said.

"Yes, it did, Miss Clevis," Dawn said. She smiled. It was a lovely smile.

Before I could thank them, an alarm sound shrieked from the gym. All heads turned.

Norman and I shouted the same words at the same time. "The reactor!"

We raced into the building and hurried to the gym. Everyone stood staring at Norman's reactor. He ran up to it and said, "Nothing to be alarmed about, folks. It's just overheating."

"What about radiation?" Sebastian asked.

"It's just a simulation," Norman said. "You don't think a kid could get his hands on uranium, do you? And you don't think I'd be stupid enough to build a real reactor, do you? I'd never put everyone in danger. Only a complete fool would think that."

Or a person with no good inside her, I realized. Ms. Hyde was capable of believing Norman would do something extremely dangerous, but I wasn't. Not me— Miss Clevis.

"A simulation?" Sebastian asked.

Norman nodded.

"So it's just like my virtual reality exhibit," Sebastian said. "It's a simulation, too. Just like yours. Just as good."

"*Just as good?*" Norman screamed. "It's a glove. It's a glove and sunglasses. That's not a simulation—that's the remains of a garage sale."

"I added some more wires," Sebastian said.

I smiled at them. They were so cute. I knelt down and thanked Rory.

"Does this mean I get an A in science?" he asked.

"For the rest of your life," I said. "Or at least through the sixth grade. As long as you earn it."

Whack!

I looked across the room. Mr. Brickner was yelling at a student and whacking his cane on a table. I walked over and put my arm around his shoulder.

"Have you tried kindness?" I asked.

He glared at me for an instant, like a goat that wanted to do damage with his horns, but I just smiled. And I kept smiling until he had no choice but to smile back. No choice at all.

Mr. Rubinitski came up to me. "You're here. I'd heard you got married."

"No, I was just out sick. You could say I wasn't myself for a couple days. But I'm fine now."

I walked back over to Dawn. "I really don't know how to thank you," I told her.

"I'm just glad I could help," she said. "And I even got a chance to be bad for a little bit."

"I guess you did. But don't start liking it, okay?"

"Don't worry," she said. "That's not the way I'm made. I don't have it in me to be bad."

"I hope I don't either." But I knew Ms. Hyde was gone. Well, not gone, but shoved back inside me with Jackie to balance her. It was scary. And it was something I was sure I'd think about a lot from now on. But not right now.

It felt so wonderful to be me again. I was exhausted,

but I still enjoyed the science fair. Norman took first place. No big surprise. Dawn got third, which was great. Sebastian got to give his mom back her glove right after the fair.

And I got to be me again. As far as I was concerned, that was pretty good.

Kids can be such monsters . . . literally!
Especially at Washington Irving Elementary. Read on for a sneak peek at
The Vanishing Vampire. . . .

I was on my way home from a movie when the dark thing fell on me. I'd been walking quickly, hurrying to the safety of home. Lewington isn't a dangerous place to live, but I'd just watched the late showing of *Creepers from the Crypt*. I couldn't fight the urge to rush through the empty streets. Images from the film chased me as I went, threatening to leap from my mind and become real.

Just one block back, I'd split up with my friend Norman. He'd headed left on Maple. I'd stayed on Spruce, walking past that huge oak whose roots were slowly breaking up the sidewalk by the vacant lot.

I heard nothing. I saw very little. Later, thinking back, I remembered the eyes and the teeth. At the time, I just knew darkness was dropping toward me.

And it wasn't only in the night; the darkness filled my mind and took me away.

The darkness inside me lifted as I woke, leaving me wondering why I wasn't in bed. I was somewhere hard and cold. There was dirty concrete beneath my fingers. I sat up slowly, feeling the world spin. I held very still, waiting for it to stop.

I stood. The world spun again, but with less force. I put one hand out and touched the rough bark of the tree.

The tree. Something dark? Something falling? I couldn't quite remember.

I turned toward home, unsure of what had happened. I'd passed out or fainted. No. "Guys don't faint," I mumbled to myself.

Behind, I heard the scraping slap of sneakers on the sidewalk. Someone was calling a name. Someone was calling me. I turned, moving cautiously, afraid that the world would follow my motion and start to spin again.

It was Norman. He was running toward me, one finger pushing up the glasses that were always sliding down his nose. "Splat, hey, Splat, you okay?"

They call me Splat. It's a long, stupid story. My name's Sebastian. Sebastian Claypool. That name is a short, stupid story. Before I was born, Mom and Dad were listening to a lot of music written by Johann Sebastian Bach. Dad thought Johann would be a strange

132

name for a kid. So, *blam*, they hang Sebastian on me. Thanks, Dad.

It could have been worse. They also liked the poet Percy Bysshe Shelley.

Norman reached me and stood there, taking deep breaths like a catfish dragged onto shore. Running was not a big part of his life. The night had grown chilly, and the air turned to swirls of fog as it left Norman's nostrils. "I looked back and you were on the ground," he said. "Did you trip?"

"I don't know." I tried to remember. "Don't tell anyone, but I think I passed out."

"Wow, that's bad. It could mean all kinds of things." He pushed up his glasses again. "You should probably get a CAT scan. I wouldn't rule out a brain tumor—though, of course, blood sugar is generally a factor in these cases, and the glucose level by itself isn't always enough of an indicator to determine—"

"Norman." I tried to stop him. Once he got going, he was like a bus rolling down a hill. If I caught him while he was just inching along, there was hope. But after he picked up some speed and really started barreling along the Highway of Fascinating Facts, there was no way to slow him down. "Hold on. I just got a little dizzy, that's all."

"What'd you eat?" he asked.

I thought back. That part of my night was clear enough. I'd had my usual popcorn—the Tub-of-Fun size that lasts about a quarter of the way through the movie. I'd washed it down with a cherry cola. Then I'd had a pack or two of caramel chews and as many of Norman's gummy eyes as he'd let me steal. Nothing there to make a kid lose touch with the world. I told Norman the list of snacks.

He seemed to be in deep thought. I imagined him running some kind of chemical tests in his mind, looking for a reaction between the assorted snacks. This could take all night. I just wanted to get home. "Look, thanks for coming over, but I'm fine."

"Are you sure?"

I nodded. Except for the dizziness, which had almost totally faded, I felt perfectly normal. Actually, I felt pretty good. Everything was starting to look very sharp and clear. As I nodded, I noticed a slight tingling on the left side of my neck. The skin below my jaw felt numb. I rubbed the spot.

"You probably should go to a doctor or something if it happens again."

"Yes, Mother," I kidded him. Having Norman for a friend was almost like having a third parent. I noticed that the tingling in my neck was going away.

"Okay." He started to leave, then said, "See you tomorrow?"

"Sure. Maybe they got some new comics at the shop. We can check that out." The tingling was completely gone. Everything felt fine.

"Great," Norman said. "I'll see you then." He turned and walked back toward Maple.

"Thanks," I called after him. As he walked away, he seemed, for a moment, to stay in sharp focus. It was almost like my eyes were some kind of zoom lens. But as soon as I was aware of it, the illusion snapped away.

I headed home. Whatever had happened was weird, *really* weird. I took my hand from my neck, squinting as I walked into the glare of a streetlight.

My fingers felt like they were still sticky from the movie snacks. That was weird. I looked down at my hand. For a second, I couldn't tell what I was seeing. The light was so bright. Then I saw it.

There was blood on my fingers.

About the Author

David Lubar grew up in Morristown, New Jersey. His books include *Hidden Talents*, an ALA Best Book for Young Adults; *True Talents*; *Flip*, a VOYA Best Science Fiction, Fantasy, and Horror selection; the Weenies short-story collections *Attack of the Vampire Weenies*, *In the Land of the Lawn Weenies*, *Invasion of the Road Weenies*, *The Curse of the Campfire Weenies*, *The Battle of the Red Hot Pepper Weenies*, and *Beware the Ninja Weenies*; and the Nathan Abercrombie, Accidental Zombie series. He lives in Nazareth, Pennsylvania. You can visit him on the Web at www.davidlubar.com.